Kennel-born

Stories

Willem Myra

THIRTY WEST
publishing house

Kennel-born: Stories

Copyright © 2018 Willem Myra

First Edition: July 2018

Cover design by Greg Leonard

Interior images by Willem Myra

Product of the U.S.A.

For more titles and inquiries, please visit:

www.thirtywestph.com

Soon you'll be ashes or bones. A mere name, at most—and even that is just a sound, an echo. The things we want in life are empty, stale, and trivial. Dogs snarling at each other.

—Marcus Aurelius, *Meditation*

Pick your poison

Kennel-born

HEIMAT

Gray. On the ground, in the air, sticking to their bloodied faces. In their eyes. Volunteers trying their best to save those under the rubble—they dig barehanded, nails broke, skin peeling, pain elsewhere. They breathe in the dusty air, these saviors, and sweat and cry and yell, "Don't give up, don't give up. Don't. Give. Up." I admire their tenacity. Sitting on the phantom of her home, a girl holds her pet cowbird to her chest and weeps. I wander aimlessly. An observant. An intruder. And for a millisecond I hate myself for thinking, *At least they had something to lose.*

HEREDITARY BUFFOONERY

1942. C. S. Lewis's *The Screwtape Letters* gets published in England. Disney's *Bambi* makes its debut. Your great-grandfather, the one there are no pictures, no portraits of, only stories, is drafted into the army. He's still a kid. They hand him a Tokarev and a vz. 24 and send him to war with close to no training. He doesn't even know who he's supposed to fight—the Germans, the Russians, maybe the British? His deployment lasts thirteen months. By the time he's back, only a pale shadow is left of him. Rachitic and ill. His left socket empty, the eye lost to someone's knife. One of the legs infected. "It's no burden," he tells those who ask him. "I'd do it again. Everything for my people." Then the infection spreads and he's taken to the capital for treatment. The doctors advise cutting off his leg. Your great-grandfather is learning to walk with a cane when the news reaches his hometown. The exiled king has succeeded in leading a coup d'état; new treaties are being penned to make friends out of the old foes. All that blood belched from your great-grandfather and his platoon—and for what? "I did it for the people," he still says; a bitter smile on his face, but refuses now to acknowledge the Other in the mirror.

1965. The year the first person walks in space. The year Allen Ginsberg's free reading prompts the creation of the International Poetry Incantation. The year your grandpa discovers himself a vigilante. He comes back from the construction site where he's been working since he dropped out of school to find his parents in tears. Inquiring around, he learns that his sister was forced to strip naked in the middle of the street by a boy three years her junior, who then "touched and kissed her *all over*." Your grandpa's parents are devastated for they know the perpetrator won't see any punishment; he is, after all, the mayor's youngest. Your grandpa is shorter than average, described by most as aloof, and has no notion of politics. That night, he pockets his lead brass knuckles and goes looking for the kid. The following morning nobody mentions the incident at the tavern, which your grandpa writes off as the rumor not having circulated yet. It's almost noon when the mayor shows up; he raises both hands comically as he tells your grandpa's father he's there in peace. Later, as the conversation moves to the living room, your grandpa overhears the first citizen says, "I intend to do everything in my power to restore your daughter's honor." That summer your grandpa's name gets purged from the wedding invitation list.

1999. THE END IS NIGH! everybody says, not just the madmen at the intersection. People are putting together supply kits, buying firearms, distrusting the Millennium-Bug-riddled computers. Not your dad. He is confident doomsday is still a good way ahead. He is confident this country will not be able to ensure you a decent future. You're six; your first school year is up. Instead of hugging you and telling you, "You're gonna do great, bud!" as you reluctantly walk inside the big, scary building, your dad quits his 6-to-11 job and meets with dubious men. Three days later he's en route to cross to the West when the van they're clandestinely riding on gets busted by the militia of a neighboring country.

Your dad and four other men run for their lives. For a week they hide in the woods, eating crabapples and soft fruits and drinking from a muddy stream, but eventually, fate turns its back on them. The militia returns with sniffing dogs; they are found, cuffed, and dragged to prison. One, two, three, four days they are left in solitary to starve. Then a lieutenant materializes inside the cell and shoves the muzzle of a gun into your dad's face. Back from school one October morning, you find your dad sitting in the kitchen. You remember his black t-shirt; so uncharacteristic. You remember the cast on his arm. You remember the circles around his eyes. The sadness lingering on his face even as he forces himself to smile at your sight.

2009. Not the year Ricky Nelson sings "Hello Mary Lou". Not the year Hamas rises to power. You have a fight with your old man because he won't let you go visit a boy met online. You're sixteen and take anarchism to heart. You sneak out of the apartment building in this Mediterranean country you've been living in for six years and get on a train—destination: love. Halfway there the train conductor decides to play the villain, and who are you to refuse to right the wrongs of this world? You try to hide, concoct a plan, but Blaine the Mono's avatar sniffs you out, chasing you through the cars until you're out of breath and decide, *That's it.* So, you face him, do your one-two, one-two dance and jab him in the face. Your young fists, harmless. An attempt to silver-tongue your cause is thwarted by cold eyes saying, *I've already heard them all.* It's a god-forgotten mountain town, the one you're kicked out at. "Your luggage, sir." In vain you tell him you didn't board with any luggage; he hands you a suitcase and the train resumes its journey.

The suitcase is empty. You don't own a cell phone, and your scarce finances neither permit you to pursue your adventure nor retreat home. The ground is cold to the touch. Above the station's decadent façade, the town's name has faded into oblivion. It's with sweaty palms covering your eyes and adolescent angst choking your synapses that you let the coughed noise slip in between your lips, unconvincingly at first, then with strength, with verve, with hatred. And again. And again. Until the platform is peopled with busybodies wondering who you are and what conspired together to reduce you to such a sorry state and why, oh why, are you now barking at the impervious sky?

FINDING A PLUMBER ON SUNDAY

Eleven towns in two days. She was burning through them, Mel was. Pure, unadulterated blandness. From first to last. A gallimaufry of repurposed Communist-era buildings still untouched by the hardships of gentrification, work-and-church people, and the ubiquitous unpaved road that bisects fields and residential areas alike. Ouf. Like, wake me up when Mr. Pique-Your-Interest knocks at the door. A break in the scenery came from a public restroom stall in the form of a PSA. The twelfth town, this was. And the afternoon of the third day. Amid graffiti of gratuitous racism and anatomically incorrect stickmen, someone had handwritten on the wall informing the world at large of his portentous talent at pleasing women by ways of tongue and jaw work alone and had concluded the message with such-and-such street and number and by inviting non-believers to test the verity of his statement. Boy howdy thought Mel.

After buckling up her pants, she asked the clerk at the pitiful little petrol station at which she'd stopped if the address was far from there, whereupon he gave her *the* look. But stubborn as she was, and bored as she was, she pressed until he finally said that no, it wasn't far, in fact, it was right around the corner, the big house with the blue fence next to the modest house with the not-so-blue fence. You can't miss it, he said. But should. Though I guess it's none of my business.

No, it's not, Mel retorted. She fumbled for a cigarette, threw up Marlboro smoke in his face. Shit. I suppose you're right. He would be a zoo of STDs, the cunnilingus guy, wouldn't he?

A walking factory, the clerk said without missing a beat.

Say, what's a gal to do to have some fun in this chewed-up bubble gum town of yours?

Well, there's a... a new pièce at the Cultural Center. "A Funny Thing Happened," I believe. If you want, I can— My shift ends at eight.

At the thirteenth town she found the streets deserted, the homes quiet. In a front yard, a mutt dragged its rear on the ground and morphed into a mountain of a shrug when interrogated regarding his owners' whereabouts. Mel took it upon herself to solve this mysterious mass disappearance. Two streets over the case were already closed. She found them in the main plaza, two or three hundred people—the town's entire population, by the looks of it. Organized in concentric circles, they were standing on the outskirts of the plaza. Men and women. Smooth-faced and wrinkled. Even teenagers, which impressed Mel.

All eyes were on a throne of sorts—an iron chair soldered atop a newspaper kiosk. On display up there, a sole man, well-dressed and well-coiffed. He wasn't talking. He wasn't smiling. All he did was a big bag of nothing. The crowd was chanting what Mel imagined to be his name, Schabowski, though she had no idea who that was. She reached for the closest person, a woman with a baby papoose to her breast, and asked about it. It's Günter Schabowski's birthday, the woman said. Met with perplexity, she explained, We owe him the freedom of our brothers. He relegated the Wall to history textbooks.

At that moment the cycles of people shifted; young boys and girls were pushed towards the middle of the plaza. Mel climbed a three-stepped staircase leading to a haberdashery to gain a vantage point. She saw a tow-headed kid reach into the front pocket of his pants, come away with an egg-sized rock. The kid hesitated, eliciting the encouragement of the grownups. Then he threw the rock at Schabowski. Five meters below, Schabowski's head encountered the cold pavement. The man grunted, forehead bloodied, but still, he rose to his feet. That's when the other kids marched in on him.

In the sea of heads and well-cultivated rage and sweating torsos, everybody began swinging, kicking, spitting. Knuckles met cartilage, shoes trampled bones, unkindness pierced flesh. The words all rose up into the sky like flocks of birds, Schabowski is dead! Long live Schabowski! Mel observed the surreal scene from afar. What was the appropriate response to bedlam? When in

Rome… she thought, before giving up on the mood.

It all lasted but a few moments. Then the kids, most of whom were in a visible state of distress, found refuge in their parents' arms. The plaza started leaking people. Mel searched for the woman with child, and, failing to find her, asked a random fellow where it was they were going. We're building a wall out of town, he said. Why? asked Mel. The man was flummoxed. How else are we going to tear down a wall if there is no wall?

The crowd evaporated. Quiet now.

A fetid breeze of tobacco and armpit hit Mel in the face. She tried averting her gaze from it; still, her focus went to the corpse left behind in the middle of the plaza. Clothes war-torn, hair a Medusa offspring. She was thinking about the next town—the fourteenth—when the corpse staved off the silence with a cough and a barely-muttered question. Did I…make them proud?

You did swell, gorgeous, Mel said getting closer. You were such a cool cat.

She got down on her knees. Caressed his cheeks. Rubbery at the touch. A doubt came over her. She probed about. That wasn't his true identity: Schabowski wore a mask. She took it off to reveal a much younger, swollen face. Chestnut hair cropped close to the scalp. Petite nose. Mel noticed a cold intelligence in his eyes. Poor man. She couldn't leave him in that state, could she? She thought about setting up a candlelight vigil to direct his soul to the heavens, a gesture so mundane and pathetic she yawned.

I'm…dying.

Yeah. Tough titty.

The plaza, the streets, the few storefronts—all deserted. The sky was transitioning to a darker hue. Mel's bony fingers trailed his rising and falling chest, unzipped his pants, reached inside. A hand job was the least a martyr like him deserved. The ultimate bliss before ad infinitum nada. She patted around only to be met by the wrong set of genitalia. More surprised than embarrassed, Mel let out a short laugh. Still, she partook in charity. Months later she'd retell the story as a parable of the human condition, saying that she sat down the entire night, eating away at the thespian's fear of death, but the truth is, by sunup, she had burned through three more towns searching for the movida that could shock her back to her senses and deliver her that much needed existential plowing.

RE: ANTIGONISH

We are grumpy larks, my wife and I. We wake up at dawn, summoned by the sun's yawns, but can't stand anybody subjecting us to their blabbering before eight, nine a.m. To avoid being a nuisance to one another, my wife puts on her fluorescent tee-shirt and rubbery shorts and goes for a run while I stay in to prepare breakfast. Sometimes I have a classic song strumming on the radio. Sometimes I give the television a chance to lie to me about the world out there. Today's the latter.

I'm spiraling the spatula through the mixture of eggs and milk when out of the corner of my eye, what do I notice? A familiar face on the screen. It's one of that scuttlebutt talk shows that nobody ever watches, and today's guest is none other than my high school best friend Osey T. We met in an extracurricular Latin class when I was fifteen. God, that feels forever ago. The teacher paired us for a translation exercise and we bonded over the silly things teenagers do, such as looking up dirty words in the dictionary.

Me: *Listen here. Vagina: (1) a sheath; (2) a scabbard; (3) a husk.*

Osey: *Yeah, a sheath for my veiny sword.*

[Cue the acne-rich laughter]

Osey wanted to become a poet, was in love with Trilussa and Montale. Unbeknownst to him, poetry doesn't sustain lifestyles—not in Italy, not outside dreamland. After graduation, I enrolled at university while he took a year off to figure out what to do next. We'd keep in touch every now and then, mostly by e-mail, and by the time I'd besieged Elisa's heart we had regressed to being pen pals. The response to my wedding invitation is the last I've heard of him.

Dude, that's huge. Congrats! I'm in Sidney, working on something, so, unfortunately, I won't be able to make it. But I wish you and the missus the best everything: *wedding, life, sex. Especially sex!*

And now here he is, on television, a rookie Pasolini discussing filmmaking and his soon-to-hit-the-theaters debut movie. Guess that sabbatical year did pay off.

When Osey's first chapbook was rejected, his father gave him a speech leading up to, *The world would starve if we were all ballerinas.* I'm glad Osey had the endurance to prove him wrong.

I turn off the television, place the plate with the omelet on the table, and when I turn back the stove is gone. Moreover, the sink is gone, as well. And the cabinets, the fridge, the microwave. Even the table with the still-steaming breakfast! That's a heart stopper.

Then it hits me: my kitchen furniture is not playing hide-and-seek. I am. And I'm hella good at it, too. One blink of an eye and I've changed zip codes. *Alex, I know this one. What is spontaneous teleportation?*

A brief glance around tells me I'm indoors. Dark walls, egg-carton decorations. A background buzz. Smells like a bedroom after you've been bed sick and haven't opened a window in days. It's an ecosystem of professional cameras on tripods, boom poles, clap lamps, diffusers. Everything pointed at a central set furnished to resemble a living room. And on the central set—

People are staring at me. A baby-faced man kneeling on the ground proceeds to take off his headphones and address me in a very authoritarian voice, the kind you wouldn't expect from what I presume to be his age. "Who are you? What are you doing here? I can't deal with any more stress right now."

I shrug. I've been my own roommate for thirty-six years, so I know if I were to open my mouth I'd ejaculate a river of nervous and mispronounced words. Instead, I point to my ensemble—the spatula and the apron that says A COOK WHO CAN GIVE TANTALUS THE HEAVE-HO—hoping it'll induce him to believe I belong to some culinary show. It does. "That's in the bungalow," the baby-faced man says. "Studio 6."

As I'm about to thank him, a fatback grassero calls security on me. Before I'm not-so-gently pushed out I glance one last time at the central set where an oblivious Osey is chatting with the over-caffeinated host.

Outside, the security guard watches me stride towards where I think Studio 6 to be. Forty-eight steps later, I turn right, out of the guard's line of sight, and I pull a Laurel-and-Hardy by ducking behind a golf cart. That's a heart racer.

The results of an unconscious brainstorming session wash over me. I've been trying to contact Osey online since—forever, really. But no matter what sort of message I come up with, it sounds pretextual, fake, more like a chore than a pleasure. I have yet to push the send button. However, now that fate dropped me back on his path, I do have a conversation starter. I'll wait for Osey to leave the building, then bump into him. I'll feign not recognizing him. *Osey? Skinny Ass Osey? Is that really you?* He'll invite me to lunch to catch up on how we wasted our youth. I'll tell him about how I've become what I despised the most—a boring teacher—and he'll explain to me, by ways of lowbrow metaphors, how he went from being the next Eminescu to the next Edgar Reitz. A sound plan. All that is left to do is wait.

Half an hour or so later, while the sun is cooking me masterfully behind this golf cart, I see Osey exiting the RAI studio. I get up and prepare myself mentally when a red flag goes up. *What's wrong?* I think. *Now, now, boss*, my reptile brain says, *where do you think you're going bare-footed in your jammies?* Shit. There's an etiquette and I was about to plow through it. I can't have Osey see me like this. I'm not socially kosher.

I hide until he leaves the premises in his expensive SUV, at which point I go back to the security guard and beg him to lend me his phone. Literally, beg him—palms folded, knees on the ground. He grunts excessively but turns out he's a good man.

"Where are we? The address, I mean." He shakes his head, probably thinking I'm some Z-list celebrity the blow has fried the neurons off and gives me the where and when. Even the year!

I wait out front, dangling my dirty toes on the sunlit sidewalk. I play the part of the bum; I even collect fifty cents. To think that this once used to be the Hollywood on the Tiber...

It's almost midday when Elisa arrives on the scooter.

"It's a tonic seeing you, my love, my savior!"

"How did you get out here?"

"I don't wanna talk about it."

"And dressed like that nonetheless?"

"Please, please take me home before I start crying."

That night I think about messaging Osey on Facebook, a quick *Hey there!* to wish him good luck with the premiere. I think about it. But I don't risk it. I'm afraid he might think I'm only interested in his newfound popularity. I can't have him replace the goofy teenager he'd tell dirty jokes to with a shallow, opportunistic prick. I'd rather our friendship fades out. Sad. Dignified. *Stercus accidit*, the Latins would say. But since they're all dead, peace to their greedy souls, what we say instead is *Shit happens*.

The next morning, back from her run, Elisa enters the house circumspectly. Her relief is palpable when she finds me on the couch in the living room, messing with my phone. "I was afraid I'd have to come pick you up in Milan," she jokes.

I don't laugh.

"Are you still indisposed?"

I shake my head. "Come, have a look at this."

She leans to peek at the screen, face lit up by curiosity. She takes in the interface of the Latin-Italian translator app. Then she notices the word vagina in bold. Curiosity turning into disbelief. Disbelief bordering on disappointment. "I'll be in the shower if you need me for non-trivial matters." And off she goes, leaving me here to giggle to myself—the foolish husband stuck in a boyish recollection.

THREE PLACES IN THE GEOGRAPHY OF US

(1)

The cul-de-sac where I got down on my knees for the first time. A decade later I have yet to meet someone unable to enjoy a blowjob like [you] on that night. [You] were so nervous, your gaze skipping around, trying to check any window, any door, any bush a person might appear from, like some jack-in-the-box ready to peep on us. I told [you] to relax, and [you] got even tenser, that tic on your right index finger resurfacing. The universe has a sick sense of humor. Recently I had to sell my car and move back to the old city. I work at a grocery store not far from our cul-de-sac. Sometimes I take smoke breaks to stare down that place and ask myself questions I will probably never find the answer to.

Questions such as: *Have other teenagers discovered the joy of oral sex in that cul-de-sac?*

Such as: *Do [you] still think about me?*

Such as: *And if so, do [you] perhaps consider us a was-that-shouldn't-have-been?*

(2)

That hotel in Barcelona we went to our senior year. The first day of vacation I got sick so [you] went searching for a *farmacia* while I stayed in, feverish. I don't think I've ever told [you] but there was a forgotten air duct in our room. A square opening barely wider than my shoulders, it had been occulted behind the nightstand, and since I wasn't sure if I was hallucinating or not, I decided to explore it. Wouldn't you know it, it led to an internal garden the size of a squash court. The Astroturf was well maintained, and, above, I could see a chunk of the sky so azure it had to have been stolen from a Miyazaki film. There were no flowers, no shrubs, only a friendly pigeon cooing in a corner. I remember sitting cross-legged on the ground, waving at the bird, questioning the reality of everything. I felt a poem: "Caged Girl" by Angelou. I felt a painting: "Lady with Dove" by Da Vinci. I felt transcendental. At some point, I must've fallen asleep because I woke up the next morning in bed. [You] never told me if [you] carried me in from the garden, or if I was already inside when [you] came back. [You] never told me if the secret passage was real or fever-induced. [You] never told me the truth, but [you] never told me lies either.

(3)

Your Nana's place back when Asia was just an all-girls band and the world could fit on a wall map. After being introduced [you] ran outside with your yellow pad and your bowl of water. "I'm busy," [you] said. Shaped like a nine-year-old yet with middle-aged worries. I asked what with and [you] proclaimed to be a biologist. "I study the rigor mortis of invertebrates. Or try to. I—I—" The words toiled to leave your mouth. "I don't have the heart to kill them myself." I, hitman by nature not nurture, put my services at your disposal. We, together, squatted by a flat stone the size of a pumpkin that had been moved aside, exposing the damp earth underneath. Ants and minute shiny bugs, a kind that audibly pops when squashed, squandered around while a fat angleworm, half buried in a hole, was wiggling its tail. I pulled it. My lack of knowledge on the matter had me question the anatomy of the invertebrates—did they have teeth to bite me with or other means of defense? Next, I wondered if I was pulling too aggressively; how much strength was *too much*, and could the worm rip in two, piñata-style? The answer never came, for I managed to unearth it quickly, then to drop it into the bowl. "Is that good?" I asked. [You] jotted down notes about the angleworm's panic dance as water slowly stuffed every hole in its maroon body. Soon the angleworm was indistinguishable from a swollen stick. As [you] described all this to future generations, I pictured spending the rest of my summer there, turning over rocks like there was a birthday present hidden beneath them. [You] giving orders; me pulling the metaphorical trigger. Long, sweaty days committing invertebrate genocides. How many micro-verses did we play Nazis with before the novelty wore off?

LETHARGY + A SKETCH ON LEGACY

She is the witness to her own murder. Her assassin is consuming her from the inside, peeling off one layer after another. It's a slow and excruciating death. The core of her being—gone. She's now defined not by what she does but by what she doesn't do. She: doesn't date anymore, doesn't blog, doesn't swim, doesn't text. Her brother notices the erosion of her personality, asks what happened. She'd like to reply with something eye-opening, something poetic, like "Social anxiety is a reverse Panopticon," but that'd sound artificial, pretentious. So instead she shrugs, adding *doesn't talk* to who she has become.

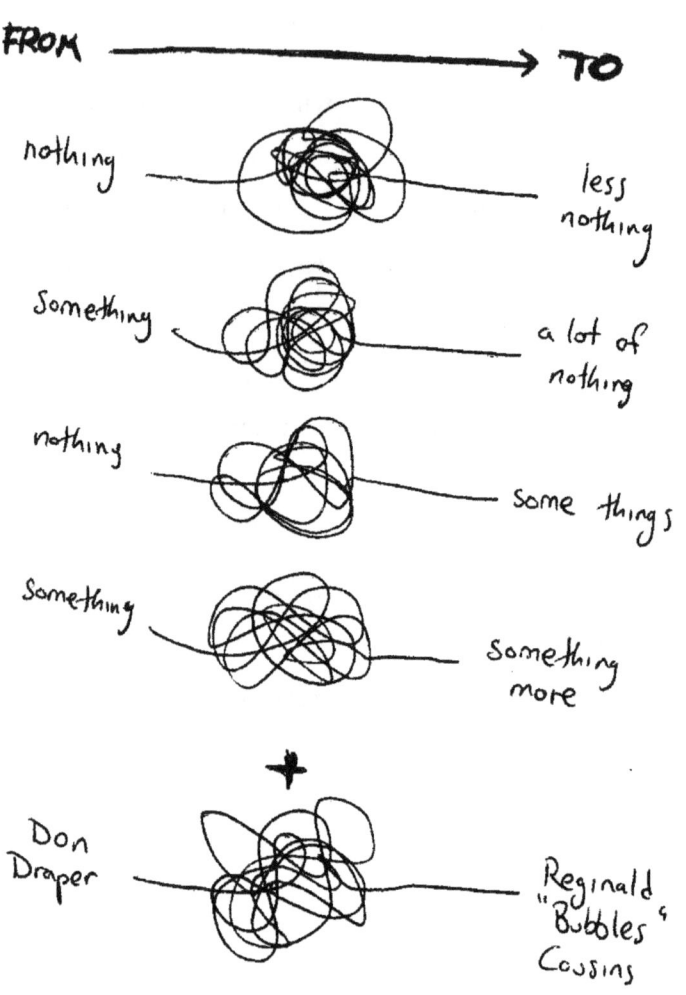

FROM ⟶ TO

nothing — less nothing

Something — a lot of nothing

nothing — some things

Something — something more

+

Don Draper — Reginald "Bubbles" Cousins

The Four Main Life Models, plus
a TV-savvy, Cross-Network Life Model

PERSEPHONE AIN'T COMIN' BACK

In this city, a nice city, a rotten city, an a-OK city if you overlook the overlookable, women are entitled to social assistance by devoting their lives to suffering. Suffering which comes in the guise of an atmospheric diving suit sans oxygen tank, massive & rusty, chaste & imposing, neither warm nor cold, a suit the woman cannot get rid of. Of course, Mother did all this for me: almost two decades she's been married to her pains so I could learn from the best eggheads her ostracized smiles could afford. *Afford to love yourself again*, I told her once I came of age, not long back. Back a maiden she is, having filed for divorce last week; a joy seeing her wear a bright color. Color me surprised when I heard her change of civil status wouldn't last. Last I saw Father I was four & now he's returned, not stranded here but on his own accord, come to finally marry his half. Half a dozen relatives & twice as many friends & neighbors crowd the wedding parlor: a garden filled with oxlips & photographers sprouting from every bush, with a one-roomed church emerging from the center of the scenery, its walls covered in stern-leaf patterns & an anatomically correct seven-foot-tall heart sitting on the roof instead of the previous outmoded ideological paraphernalia the architect had wanted: crosses & obese men & pasta & such. Such a dreamy day, such a fuzzy atmosphere. *Atmosphere, stratosphere, exosphere, don't make me fear!* Mother's diving suit, removed from her & high on loneliness, blabbers to whoever pays it any attention, which isn't many. Many applaud as the trumpets sing & the bride descends the marble staircase with confident accomplishment, the veil only coming down to her watery eyes. Eyes samba back & forth from her to the groom. Groom holding her hand—not really The Groom, rather a placeholder: a tall man in a tuxedo with a paper bag slid on. On the paper bag, someone's handwritten a name: Father's. Father's by my side, or at least what's left of him. Him, gone for all my life, working abroad like a banshee in hopes of being reunited with us on this day. Day in, day out of just going at it. It being a sacrifice. Sacrifice being hard. Hard to wrap my

mind around the fact that only a leg's left of him—
a complete leg at that, bone + flesh + hair,
kneecap → toes. *Toes,* Mother's diving suit says,
then corrects itself: *Toast!* it shouts, failing to have
anybody join in. In trying to cultivate his finances,
the rest of his body Father burnt out or pawned
or had to give up on. On paper, only a leg is left
of him; that & an eye. Eye which I bear in my right
socket, so not really his anymore. More than a
lifetime ago I lost my original right eye in a childish
wage at the, you guessed it, nursery. Nursery
rhymes Grandma mutters seeing her little girl in
white. *White trash, family wrecker, chickenshit:* words
Grandpa would use in conjunction with the
subject *thou* when addressing me as a kid, hence
why he wasn't invited today. Today Father & I are
shadows occupying the outskirts of the garden;
today it is not our day; today we are not
protagonists. Protagonists of the photos being
snatched: Mother & her radiant rebirth & her
mesmerizing dimples & her bouquet. Bouquet
high in the sky. Sky filled with heavy, rusty,
anachronistic jumping women appeared today

hoping to see in Mother a glimpse of their future manumission. *Manumission (man-yuh-mish-uh) from Latin:* manūmittēre *(to put hand)*, the diving suit tells me & when I look beyond the thick glass viewport I see it's in such a sorry mess, I can't but offer to hug it. It refuses, instead of going around wailing in a wine-rich voice, *I need her, I need her, I need her!* Her inhabiting now a different reality, not here but there. *There ought to be a moral to this, right?* I ask Father. Father says, *Probably not*, or would say so were he to have a mouth, which he doesn't, so instead he contracts his big toe & digs a tailored grave in the fresh earth.

DAZAI HOTEL

One.

Miss Belte from 209 has an affair with Mr. ████ from ██. That's at the Dazai Hotel. Only the two of them know about it. The two of them and The Creep, for The Creep has cameras installed throughout the entire place—perks of being a bellhop.

Miss Belte is a recluse. A guest for nineteen days, she's never left the hotel once. She has her meals delivered to her room, and when in need of small comforts—junk food, off-the-record Hennessey, the occasional paperback—she bribes either The Creep or TOLDB (The Other Less Deviant Bellhop) to do her bidding. She spends her days watching TV and listening to music on her laptop, though it is not unusual to see her doing yoga on the mahogany table in the living room. The Creep's got thirteen low-res, black-and-white screenshots of her doing Downward Facing Dog and Bound Angle on his phone.

The second gotchi-goo Mrs. ████ goes window shopping, Mr. ████ invites Miss Belte over. This is the only time she leaves her room. Before sneaking to the ▮▮ floor, she changes into her sexy lingerie, applies abundant makeup and perfume, and hollows herself out. This she does by uncapping one of her big toes and letting the water pour out of her and into the bathtub. The golden flounder inhabiting her ribcage also slips out. She pats its murky scales with the tip of a bony finger and whispers something to it—to behave, The Creep surmises, though the recording does not come with audio. Then she's off to her escapade.

If The Creep is off-duty or if there's nothing impellent for him to do, he takes it upon himself to keep her flounder company. Such a romantic bozo. He lets himself into the room with the cloned card and sits on the floor by the bathtub. The flounder swims in circles as he reads aloud Japanese existential novels off his phone. Every so often he checks on the live feed from Mr. ▮▮'s bedroom so that he knows when to leg it. Some days The Creep takes out his own golden flounder, though he never allows the two fish to come into contact. Instead, he vomits it into a glass of water which he then places on the border of the bathtub. The flounders love to study each other from afar as if to try and understand which one's the exhibit and which the visitor. This The Creep calls "soulgazing".

Miss Belte's post-escapades follow the same routine. Once back, she gets naked and inert in front of the bathroom mirror, faces an unflinching mask, sobs tight-lipped. Afterward, she grabs a straw and drinks herself full again. What little water is left on the bottom of the bathtub that she can't suck in, she lets go down the drain. Lastly, she picks the flounder by the tail and swallows it in a flame eater motion, avidly chewing as she does.

Two.

Music you can talk over plays in the elevator when Mrs. ▮▮▮ comes in. 10:30 on the dot. A creature of habit.

"Hot day, huh?" asks The Creep.

"If it keeps like this we might go down to the beach."

"Second week of the honeymoon?"

"Third."

"Wow. Congrats on...having that kind of money, I guess."

Mrs. ███ gives a polite laugh.

"Lobby?"

"Yes, thank you."

As the doors close, The Creep starts juggling with the three cans of dog food he's carrying. She asks if they're for his pet, to which he replies not really. Then he drops a can on the floor.

"Let me help you."

With her stooped over, he pushes the emergency button, forcing the elevator to come to a halt, and clunks her over the head with a can. She lets out but a yelp.

The Creep overrides the elevator's controls, sending it to the basement. Here he grunts Mrs. ███ to a chair he's previously set up, ties her arms and legs in a sitting position and gags her. The basement is seldom visited by the hotel staff, being more of a storage for the dozen vending machines the original owner bought before dementia caught up with him. A single light bulb dangles from the ceiling. A plastic, roundtable accompanies the chair. The Creep empties his pockets, placing on table two yellow envelopes. One contains the photographs of the affair; the other a shit-ton of bills— seventy percent of his life savings to be precise. Stored underneath his clothes, between wife beater and uniform, are the divorce papers, already filled out and in need of her signature. The math is simple.

The Creep navigates the maze of vending machines rehearsing the women-empowering little speech he's prepared about infidelity and starting over, every so often glancing at gotchi-goo Mrs. ██ and wondering how much longer until she comes to her senses.

Except Mrs. ██ never comes to her senses.

Three.

His father was a techie by craft. The old man had this proverb framed over his desk: *Whenever you struggle to wrap your spine 'round a problem, remember that there's probably, most definitely, bloody certainly an app for that.*

Indeed, The Creep finds what he needs on the online store: a detective app game overflowing with ideas. Browsing through the scenarios in which the perpetrator must dispose of the victim without leaving behind clues of foul play, he notices one suitable to his current impasse. It's no easy labor to drag Mrs. ██████ to the elevator, or out of it, or through half a floor. He's close to the door leading to the roof when someone clears their throat behind him. He finds TOLDB staring from the other end of the hallway. All the pink runs out from The Creep's face. He knows he should do something, can't come up with anything. TOLDB sighs. "When the badges will inevitably come sticking their fingers in your disgusting pie," he mutters, "I will plead zero foreknowledge. You try to incriminate me in any capacity, even as a simple witness, and I'll fuck you up beyond imagination." With that, he heads downstairs.

From the roof, The Creep checks the main entrance to the hotel, the streets and alleyway surrounding it. All clear. Soaked in sweat, he employs his last ounce of energy to lay Mrs. ██████'s body on the ledge, then he pushes it down. He refuses to watch the aftermath, only hears the thud. The splash. The female shriek that follows closely thereafter.

By the time a crowd has gathered around the corpse, he's in the street, too, cursing the gods and sobbing and hating himself for having to put on such a charade. Though he's moved by love, and that, he knows, is enough to have his actions forgiven. His *is* a just cause.

Four.

As the medical workers are about to bag her, Mrs. ██████ comes back to life. Can you hear that? That's the sound of a certain someone shitting his pants. Mrs. ██████ makes her way through the shocked crowd, approaches a dumbstruck Creep, and goes on a bitch-slapping frenzy yelling, "You did this to me, you did this to me, you did this to me," until his head disconnects from his neck. Then leaking-goo Mrs. ███ returns to the point of impact of her body with the concrete, lies down on the ground, shakes her arms and legs just so in the mixture of blood, brains, and other bodily fluids—a macabre snow angel the coroner has the audacity to call art.

Coda.

The cameras in room 209 are off with one exception. The surviving electronic eye is not where The Creep installed it; has been repositioned to frame the empty bathtub on whose bottom awaits a message in lipstick: THANKS FOR THE READINGS ;). Lying in the hospital bed, The Creep picks up his phone, the one the police failed to take away and calls room ███. The uncuffed hand reaches downwards. "Hello?" Miss Belte's angelic voice pierces his lateral orbitofrontal cortex. The Creep melts into heavy breathing, into self-complacency.

AN INTOXICATED MASCOT'S RAMBLINGS

One evening while dining alone at a *yatai*[1], the author of this report was approached by a man wearing a Lunatic Laszlo costume[2] which led to the two of them becoming drinking pals. For the entire night, ideas and beer brands were explored. Backstories, too. The following is a verbatim transcript[3] of the salient monologues of that night. The punctuation alone belongs to the author.

§

10 PM. Two of my friends died in accidents here. [*Pointing across the street.*] Right here. They were the lucky ones. All my other dead friends? Not much of an accident. But I'm a'ight, no need for worry. I'd never kill myself. I've got this. [*Meaning the Lunatic Laszlo costume.*] This is one tank of a mask.

---

[1]   A Japanese street food vendor usually selling noodles.
[2]   Lunatic Laszlo is the mascot for a chain of fast food restaurants the author doesn't feel comfortable mentioning by name giving the recent (2016-ish) allegations. Lunatic Laszlo is a large, yellow-legged creature resembling a dodo bird with an elongated beak and a floppy hat.
[3]   Typed on a computer from memory the day after the events thanks to the author's hyperthymesia condition.

10:16 PM. At fifteen I had a premonition of what was to come. [*Chuckles revisiting memories.*] I studied Dad and his friends and I knew my future was going down the drain. I panicked. So I tried to summon Satan. [*Tosses down an entire beer can.*] Candles, chalk pentagram, reciting his name while staring in a mirror all Bloody Mary-like. I went with the whole package. Such a lame-o. As a result, nothing happened. Incidentally, the following day, which was Saturday, a friend of mine came by. He was holding a cucumber. I asked him, "Why are you holding a cucumber?" He said, "This cucumber here has the solution to everything." "How so?" I asked. "See," he explained, "when cleaning it earlier this morning, I must've rubbed it the right way 'cause a genie came out of it." "Get outta here," I said. "No, no, it's true. A genie willed itself into existence and is to grant me three wishes. But you know how these things go, there's always a loophole somewhere, a trick that effs you just so you get out of it worse than you went in. I wanna avoid that."

10:23 PM. He came up with a plan. [*The cook serves a new bowl of beef ramen noodle soup.*] Long story short, my friend believed that if he befriended the genie first and foremost, the genie would then think twice before fucking him over. Sort of like how you try and tell your kidnapper personal things in hope of creating a connection. And my friend's idea for befriending the genie was to give up two of the three wishes. The first would go to me, so he'd appear kindhearted. My friend would take the second, though not before telling the genie that the third wish would go to him.

10:27 PM. Thoughtful pauses prevailed all my life. I can already see it. My eulogy: "Died of thoughtfulness."

11:42 PM. My friend wished for infinite knowledge of the law so that he could one day open a good firm and become successful and rich. The genie, of course, wished to be liberated from his predicament. Me? I did a dumb.

11:44 PM. [*He strips down to his tighty-whities and mismatched socks but keeps the head of Lunatic Laszlo on. He relieves himself on a public building.*] Have you ever heard the one about the nomad and the farmer? After a whole day of walking, a nomad bumps into a farmer. The farmer looks down at the tired nomad and spits into his face. Incredulous, the nomad thanks the farmer for his generosity in times of harsh drought.

12:09 PM. Wanna know how the genie phrased it? He said, "Thus far I've been a verb to many. From now on I wish to be but a noun for myself." A motherfucking poet that dude was.

1:37 AM. There are monsters roaming our streets. Their creed is inequality. They spit and curse and punch everything that's not like them. I'm afraid I'll encounter a bunch of these monsters who'll think I'm rooting for the wrong soccer team. Do you ever fear that, friendo? You ever fear to be unable to get your point across?

2:15 AM. Apologies for being a downer. I get sour by the hour after sundown. Here, drink up, drink up. The tab's on me

2:16 AM. [*Observes a deli worker standing under an awning, looking at the posters announcing the start of the rodeo season.*]

4:50 AM. I wish crying came easy. No, that's not what I asked the genie for. What I asked is...Let's say the media got me good. Back then there was all this talk about the West having reached an unprecedented level of prosperity. So I thought, I want to be a part of that, I want to live close to progress, to be among the first to experience the new chthonic gods that reign over microchips and Cloud. But now, now— Where the fuck's the paradise at, yo?

4:59 AM. [*Looks at the assortment of empty beer cans around him. Smacks his lips. Drinks another.*]

5:05 AM. I didn't want roots. That's what I wasted my wish on. I thought a future stems from a past, so to avoid becoming like Dad and his pals, I had to forgo *mine*. America inspired me. I told the genie, I have no history, only a frontier. How utterly blockheaded I was in my understanding of the self. The lack of a past left me empty. I'm no chameleon; I'm whatever the room I'm in needs. I can't keep onto people, for I'm a different person with each of them. *One, No One and One Hundred Thousand.* If you were to meet me tomorrow, you too, friendo, would not recognize me. Who I am now is just what you lack tonight. Capital I, in a solipsistic way, does not exist.

5:08 AM. I love that paradox. "All Athenians are liars," says an Athenian. [*Hiccups.*] If I don't have a past anymore, how was I able to tell you about it tonight? [*Begins laughing a nasty laugh.*]

5:09 AM. [*Keeps laughing.*]

5:15 AM. [*Keeps laughing.*]

5:46 AM. [*Farts without apology.*]

5:50 AM. [*Keeps laughing.*]

5:58 AM. Have you heard the one about death riding a black bull? [*He produces a beer keg from nowhere.*] Scratch that. [*Proceeds to down it all in one go.*] I have one sole wish, friendo. I want to be so fucked up I pass out awake.

CARPATHIA

Tummo drinks himself sick and silly on bodybuilding culture, so he turns the barn into a professional gym he hits seven days a week, no split workouts—every day is biceps/triceps/shoulders/chest day. Under the hood of an abandoned tractor now devoted to the beaux arts rests his treasure: powdered whey and casein protein, powdered creatine, powdered BCAAs, powdered vitamins & Omega-3, and his equally-powdered maid. The maid, Mrs. Luvina, has been accompanying him everywhere since she died of heart failure, thirteen years back. Mrs. Luvina was the mother his mother chose for him.

Aside from the minutiae he blends, Tummo enjoys a diet of meat he personally tends to. At the farm he raises seven hens; one rooster; a dozen baby chickens; three old cows, one of which is presently mother to a skinny calf; and one stubborn, soon-to-be-put-down bull. The previous tenants left behind two pigs Tummo has transformed into chipolata for the occasional cheat meal. Fiber and carbohydrates, he gets from the crops and trees growing around town.

By day he works the field, fatigues in the barn, reads *soan bungaku* books to keep his mind on par with his physique. At 6 PM, dinnertime, Tummo chats with his only friend, The Kid-Moo-Moo. Tummo tries teaching him the human tongue— grammar and syntax, puns and curses. The Kid-Moo-Moo has yet to blur a word, sign of the stubbornness inherited from his father, Tummo is sure.

8 PM through 2 AM is sleep time. Two testosterone-rich cycles necessary for muscle growth, plus a bit of REM. At 2:30 AM, after two liters of water and a handful of Steely Dan songs on full blast, Tummo grabs the shovel and goes to the graveyard. He owns the graveyard. In fact, he owns everything in this Carpathian town Ancestry.com claims to be the cradle of his predecessors, the place where his blood came from. Tummo acquired it to make right to Paleolithic mistakes. See, at the time when his grand-grand-folks lived here, a fear of *strigoi*

plagued the area, so each corpse was buried with a wooden stake through the heart. Tummo considers this a lack of respect, an obstacle to the soul's eternal rest. Every night he unearths a coffin, extracts the stake from the well-preserved body, and covers it back. Thirty-three wooden stakes lay in a corner of the barn, bearing witness to his bona fide cause, motivating him to get stronger yet so that he may soon free all the graveyard's denizens.

Tonight the wind bends the dogwoods in the dark. Tummo shovels away earth as the Kid-Moo-Moo munches sheepishly on a lost leaf. The coffin is musky, creaky. Inside, a woman's face: eyes wide and mouth agape, a scream congealed in time like "Guernica". Tummo pulls at the stake with all his might. The hole in the corpse's chest pops itself full again. The corpse sighs, relieved. With warp speed the she-*strigoi* leaps forward, intent on ripping out Tummo's jugular. He dodges the attack and, still holding firm on the wooden stake, goes to impale the *strigoi* in the sternum. His wrist in a thumb-index hold. Stalemate. Human-animal and undead stare each other in the eye. She hisses. He sweats cold. Then the she-*strigoi* lets his arm go, wrinkles into a coyote, flees in the pallid night.

"God bless you," Tummo says, his voice trembling. "Now that was some thirst for life."

He rummages through his backpack, empties a two-liter bottle of water. Afterward, he delivers himself a corny pep talk. He rolls up his sleeves, eeny-meeny-miny-moes the next grave to liberate.

"You poor, roostered son-of-a-bitch," the Kid-Moo-Moo mutters to the wind not thirty meters away.

NAUGHTY YOU DOT COM

Halfway through summer, you receive an e-mail with the subject line: YOUR WEBSITE IS LIVE & VIEWS ARE ALREADY PEAKIN. Knowing that (1) you aren't what others might describe as 'internet savvy' and that (2) you've never commissioned a website, you decide the e-mail is either spam or a scam. Still, you click it open—the skin-crawling necessity to know has driven your entire existence on this planet; as a kid your moniker was Kitty, and although others, grownups mostly, found it endearing, you truly were afraid one day this curiosity of yours would land you into an Agatha Christie-like mystery that would get you killed. But, alas, against the high-inducing aha moment, fear alone could never do much, so even as an adult, you are Wilde's brother-in-thought: you can resist everything but temptation.

The e-mail reads as such: *There are no friends nor foes in business. Only opportunities. We value our effort $3,000. We're big fans, so if you ask nicely we will let you talk us down a couple hundred. Hit us back ASAP!*

Followed by a link to a name-surname-dot-com sort of website you are disciplined enough not to click. Instead, you Google the name, finding out that Merilin Amore AKA Norma Lover AKA Priscilla from Perugia is a US-based Italian adult film star. Interesting. And what's even more interesting is that—holy moly Merilin looks just like you if you wore a tad bit more makeup and carried yourself in an attractive-person way. The discovery leaves you speechless. You have a doppelganger. A doppelganger who engages in dogging habits. A doppelganger who receives more love in a day than you managed to beg for in a lifetime. The thought plummets you into depression, then into despair. You start panicking. What if your family and friends find out about it? You conjure back the e-mail and check the sender's name. A customized domain. You question the web, coming up with words such as 'cybersquatting', 'domain squatters', 'brandjacking', and many more web-related portmanteaux. Multiple articles and forum postings paint an unfriendly picture of those who contacted you. They prey on emerging pornstars, registering domains in their name and then, as the actresses begin building a following and want to create an online home for their work, demanding not indifferent sums of money in exchange.

You finally click the name-surname-dot-com website link. The homepage is you—or, the other you—fully naked, sitting on a black background, legs apart and the word ENTER superimposed over your/her clean-shaven genitalia. How could you turn down such an invitation? Inside you're met by a classical porn website layout. A wall of videos, four per line for about—you scroll, scroll, scroll, scroll, scroll down—forty or fifty lines. The other you sure is a hard-worker. The cybersquatters must've Google-reverse-image-searched Merilin's headshot and ransack through all the social media profiles not directly connected to the industry. They were either looking for Merilin's real name or trying to maximize their profits by blackmailing every girl resembling her. Are you the first one they've e-mailed? The first one who hasn't replied yet?

After dinner, you sit in front of your computer and press PLAY on one of her scenes. You watch it in its entirety: 23 minutes and 40 seconds. You take in the eagerness, the dedication, the enjoyment. You wonder if that's how you sound when speaking; if that's how you make love, minus the experience; if that's how you moan. You feel like an ogler. You're fascinated. You put on the second video and race your doppelganger to orgasm. You win, too, but, then again, you don't have a contractual minute-count to oblige. It's almost midnight when you make up your mind. You copy-paste Merilin's showcase website and send the link to every single one of your thirty-nine Facebook friends. You preface it with a short message: *Hey, X. I've been working hard on this side-project and I'd love for you to give me some feedback. Thanks.*

Once you're finished, you prepare yourself a sandwich and devour it with gusto while flicking through the television channels. After the meal, you get on Twitter, where you have twelve followers, and tweet: *My FB account has been compromised. Don't click anything I send you. Will deal w/ it ASAP.* You spend the night awake waiting to see who will message you first to say that they thought they knew you, but boy were they fucking wrong. Tomorrow, you think with rediscovered resolve as you doze off, tomorrow I'm stepping outdoors.

DEFINE: "G O D"

God is a wishy-washy Wittgenstein beetle trapped in a shoebox under my bed. On days when could-be opportunities abort me, I take the lid off and squish Him dead. I wet my pants as I hear God pop, purple goo bursting everywhere. The following morning He's back in, a grey dot in a sea of grape-colored pimples—mementos of previous sin washings.

God is the hand-me-down bicycle I always ride in this world filled with carborne people.

God is a turgid nipple on my fiancée's survivor breast. At night I cup Him with my lips, and, suckling, I swim against life's current back to that snowy morning in the late eighties when we let our animal instincts have the best of us, and in the name of the then-misunderstood idea of democracy, we intoned MORITURI TE SALUTANT! as we drove a cannonball through Baldie and his dictatorial wife.

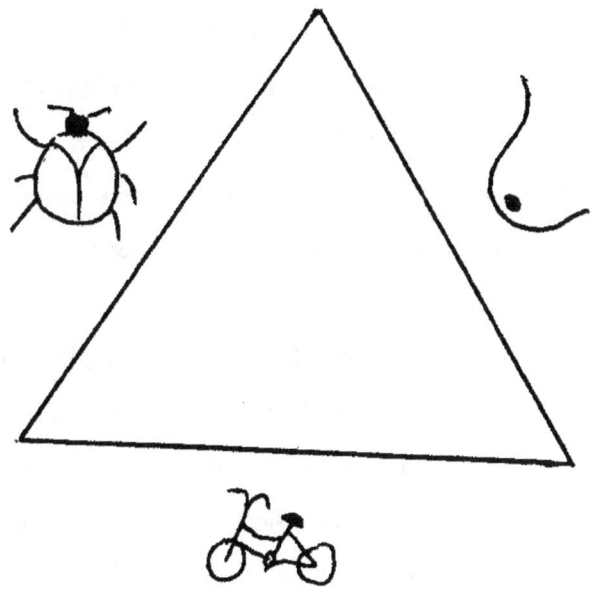

Masterful rendition of the Holy B Trinity

THE STAGE OF THE SPIRIT

The Magician announces that he's going to make the man disappear. That Pallid Fellow Over There, who volunteered for the act, sits on a chair at the center of the stage. All lights are pointed on his sweaty brow. He smiles shyly and waves at the people he came to see the show with.

Are you ready, the Magician asks with more eagerness than Busta Rhymes' passion for hip-hop. That Pallid Fellow mutters affirmatively. Ladies and gentlemen, says the Magician now facing the audience, may the show begin!

The Flirty Assistant—blond, thirty-two-teeth smile, stockings—makes her entrance pushing a man-sized mirror on wheels. She arranges it in such a way that both That Pallid Fellow and the audience can look into it. She bows, The Flirty Assistant, giggles, then is off.

The lights get low. The background atmosphere music nobody was aware of shifts into a suspenseful beat. The Magician pronounces the magic words. Sim sala bim! Or magicabula bibbidi bobbidi bu! Or some other funny-sounding made-up phrase. The surface of the mirror starts trembling like wind-caught sheets. There's a flicker. There's some static. And just like that, the mirror turns into a window on universes twins with our own. Everybody in the audience is speechless. That Pallid Fellow watches as other versions of himself appear on the enchanted screen one at the time. They are different from one another, these look-alikes. There's one who is dressed better. One who is chubbier. One is a father. One suffers from bruxism. One lost an eye. One has a wicked smile. One shakes hundreds of hands at a public event. One has a husband.

Our Pallid Fellow studies them, bug-eyed and incredulous. How are they me, how is this possible, what? he would like to shout, but doesn't, for he is an educated gentleman and knows how to keep his cool even when the fabric of reality crumbles.

The Flirty Assistant comes back followed by eight equally flirtatious girls, each of whom is pushing a wobbly wooden wheeled table. On each table sits an old-school, red, rotary-dial telephone.

Not a cordless, yet wireless nonetheless. The girls arrange the red telephones around Our Pallid Fellow and conclude the task by lifting their left legs in the air like they're '50s movie stars and they've just passionately kissed the square-jawed main character.

This is what I want you to do, says the Magician. One of the phones is going to ring. Drin, drin, drin—just like that. I want you to pick up and have a chat with your doppelganger. One at a time. Does that sound good to you?

When the telephone does eventually ring, Our Pallid Fellow picks up with confidence. Hello, he says. Yeah, that's also *my* name. By god, certainly. And it's all we and the audience hear, for the Magician has the control room cut off the sound. Let's give him some privacy, all right, fellas, the Magician says. He now sits in the front row, enjoying the show like he's an Average Joe himself.

The phone call lasts ten minutes, give or take, leaving Our Pallid Fellow ghastlier, sweatier. A second telephone starts ringing right away. And twenty minutes later, a third. Then a fourth. A fifth. And so on, until Our Pallid Fellow has shared anecdotes with all his parallel selves.

It's past midnight. Everyone is silent and attentive. Not one blinking eye. Not one yawning mouth. Our Pallid Fellow stands up, staring ahead. Arms hanging loosely. Sloping Victorian shoulders. He stares mutely, like a kitten who's seen a shadow moving on the wall. And stares. And stares. Every so often Our Pallid Fellow licks his lips, swallows saliva. His pupils follow a ceiling-to-ground then left-to-right pattern. He's a flesh-made machine. After three days of doing this, he whispers a single word—Usurper—shakes his head, and lies down on the stage in the fetal position.

Some Pallid Fellow sleeps for a whole week during which the audience stays seated and awaits. The denouement is close, you can actually smell it. When A Pallid Fellow wakes up, he isn't himself anymore. He stares in the mirror, but he does not see doppelgangers. All he sees is a skin-and-bones man wearing a dirty white tee-shirt, with a scraggly beard, uncombed hair, and a know-it-all grin.

My name is John Doe no more, the Man says, introducing himself to the audience for the first time. He makes an elegant curtsy, left hand on his belly, right one in the air; ankles crossed.

The NOW IT'S THE RIGHT TIME FOR AN APPLAUSE, THANK YOU VERY MUCH! sign bleeds red and does so for a long, long time. The audience is happy to clap louder than anybody ever did, for the Magician has indeed made the man disappear as they knew him. Bravo, bravo, bravo, comes a sea of voices from the seats. The Magician gets on stage, bows respectfully too.

Once the one-trick show comes to an end, the audience disperses. Some of them see the performance as a conversation starter to use next time they're in an awkward situation; some, poor souls, forget about it before hitting the bed. Others, however, strip naked and, in their dimly-lit bathrooms, pray their half-body mirrors to show them who they could've turned into, to show them their best selves, their lesser selves, their not-quite-themselves-but-almost selves. But the mirrors, it is known, are stubborn beings, deaf to human desires. Therefore they show nothing, sucking in all the light and turning black. SMOOTH PIECE OF GLASS THAT REFLECTS IMAGES TEMPORARILY OUT OF SERVICE. WE APOLOGIZE FOR THE INCONVENIENCE.

Bummer, The Naked People think before sighing in unison. They shake the mirrors to no avail. They are left alone, craving a once-in-a-lifetime metamorphosis, yet lacking the know-how to jump-start it. Caged inside their incompletion.

HOMO HOMINI LUPUS

Men with unclean lips brought steel bats and hatchets, handguns and rifles. But the hounds were quick and sly, already acquainted with the taste of metal, so more men than beasts succumbed on the first, second, and third week. On the fourth, propaganda-fueled megaphones cried for help. Ordinary people came to the rescue; they fashioned improvised arms from household items, fought the hounds, dreamed of utopias. Not the Sisters. The Sisters watched the civil war unfold from their footbridge-cum-house. They'd never had any trouble petting anybody.

One morning the conflict was headline news; the next it was history. After political stability was restored and the leftover hounds domesticated, with interbreeds being employed abroad in circumstances befitting their dimwits, the GUS (Government of the Undivided State) began the act of proscription. The Sisters' door knocked an ill-omened knock. On the other side, a committee of three men: one directed interrogative potshots, one took notes, the other shadowed the first two.

I've got it on record, the questioner said, that when the time came to pick sides, you picked none. Please explain yourself.

We didn't want to be associated with the wrong crowds, the Sisters said. We are not here to make friends and we are not here to make enemies. We keep to ourselves.

The note taker took notes; the shadow whispered vague threats.

Your choice could've negatively impacted the course of the entire Western History. You could've condemned us all.

The Sisters scuffed. We wish we had Aesop's disability to see such a simple world.

A week later the committee returned. Joining them were Humvees and law enforcement agents.

On behalf of the GUS, I'm to inform you that you've been declared *personae non gratae*. A fencesitter country this is not.

Tied like Andromeda to a DNA they couldn't contest, the Sisters got deported to the Cimmerian country from which their fathers originated. A land of thatched roofs and rocky enclaves. A land whose irate language left them incommunicado. A land plummeted in the dark, yet devoid of stargazers.

Panhandling. Piquing the locals' uneasiness. Forgetting their speech had sound. Dotting bribes and favors and mack-friendly winks and nods.

Ten years crawled by.

By the time the Sisters' dépaysement had faded, an aura of things colliding engulfed the country. Factions arose based on dialects. Wizened by their previous experience, the Sisters had made up their minds to never be ambivalent, never opinion-less, never *super partes*. They picked a faction and stuck to it. In the months that followed, they fought alongside their cousins and they regarded their dialect as important enough to die for. They emerged victorious. The Cimmerian country saw unity under a sole jargon.

One night in the post-ceasefire, the Sisters party in the plaza with their compatriots, hobnobbing and dancing and forgetting that their best years have passed them by, when a terribly roundy little man says, Something's not right here.

He stops petting his tomcat, takes out a pistol, then shoots one of the Sisters in the chest. Much better, the man announces, and everybody laughs and everybody dances and everybody keeps having a great time.

Blood bubbling on her lips, the wounded Sister looks up from the ground and demands to know, What for? What for? What for? Though an answer never comes.

~Fin~

Acknowledgments

Grateful appreciation is made to the publications in which first appeared, albeit with slight changes, the following stories:

"Heimat": published as "Aftermath" in *Microfiction Monday Magazine* (51st Edition); "Lethargy": published in *101 Words*; "Naughty You Dot Com": published in *Bird's Thumb*; A previous draft of what later became Chapter One of "Dazai Hotel" was published as "Drained" in *The Airgonaut*.

This book could not be possible without Florin and Eugenia. I owe you big time.